In a Heartbeat
Based on a True Story

In a Heartbeat
Ingram Noble

Note for Producers:

Publication of this play does not imply availability for performance. Both amateurs and professionals considering a production are strongly advised in their own interest to apply to Ingram Noble at ingramjnr@icloud.com for written permission before starting rehearsals, advertising or booking a theatre.

Important Billing and Credit Notes:

All producers of 'IN A HEARTBEAT' must give credit to the author (Ingram Noble) in all programmes distributed in connection with the performance of the play, and in all instances in which the title of the play appears for the purposes of advertising.

For Lila

CHARACTERS:

MICHELLE
FARRAH/PC HENDERSON
EMILY
MATT
TAYLA
NEWS REPORTER
PC ELLIOTT

ONE

TAYLA: Stop all of the clocks, cut off the telephone. Prevent the dog from barking with a juicy bone. Silence the pianos and with muffled drum. Bring out the coffin and let the mourners come.

MATT: Let aeroplanes circle overhead. Scribbling on the sky, the message – she is dead. Put crepe bows around the public doves. Let the traffic policemen wear black cotton gloves.

MICHELLE: She was my North, my South, my East and West. My working week, and Sunday rest. Our noon, our midnight. Our talk, our song. I thought that friendship would last forever. I was wrong.

EMILY: The stars are not wanted now; put out everyone. Pack up the moon and dismantle the sun. Pour away the ocean and sweep away the woods; For nothing now can ever come to any good.

TAYLA: W.H Auden.

TWO
Michelle, Farrah and Emily's house

> *(Michelle is loading a wash into the washing machine.)*

MICHELLE: Emily! Hurry up! You're going to be late for school!

> *(Farrah enters.)*

FARRAH: All right! All right! Calm yourself woman.

MICHELLE: Where's your sister?

FARRAH: I dunno.

MICHELLE: Well get yourself up those stairs and pull her out her bed – I swear to fuckin' God Farrah.

FARRAH: Calm down.

MICHELLE: Tell me to calm down one more time Farrah, I dare you.

FARRAH:

MICHELLE: Go and get your sister, or so help me God.

> *(Farrah exits.)*

MICHELLE: Fuckin' hell. Fuckin' kids, eh?

2

(Michelle sits on top of the washing machine. First, she notices the audience and then she speaks to them.)

MICHELLE: Oh hello! I'm Michelle. That was my oldest daughter, Farrah. Welcome to my House. I'm sorry I didn't clean up or anything – I didn't know you were coming or I'd have made an effort, you know. I've got two kids you see, two teenage girls and it's hard to keep on top of everything with two teenage girls in the House. A can't wait until the night when I can ship them off to their Dad's for the weekend. Two whole fuckin' days of peace before the riots start again. That's the only perk to being divorced from their Dad. Or the Ginger Prick as a like to call him – shipping those two off. Don't get me wrong, I love them more than anything in this entire world but dealing' with two hormonal girls and trying to juggle a full time job as a single Mother is hard.

(Farrah enters and Michelle stands up.)

MICHELLE: Where's your sister?

FARRAH: She's brushing her teeth, calm down!

MICHELLE: What did I just tell you?

FARRAH: Jesus Christ.

3

MICHELLE: Go and wait outside – get out of my sight
            and Marie will be here to get the both of
            you in a minute anyway.

FARRAH: Can I sit in the car?

MICHELLE: Do whatever ye want Farrah; just get out a
            ma sight.

FARRAH: Well, can a have the keys?

MICHELLE: After last time? Absolutely no chance. How
            stupid do you think I am?

            (Farrah exits.)

MICHELLE: *(Shouting)* Emily, you've got five seconds
            to get your arse out this door.

            (Emily enters.)

EMILY: Am here. Am here. Calm down woman!
            You'll give yourself' a heart attack and me
            a headache.

MICHELLE: Fuckin' move.

EMILY: I need my bag.

MICHELLE: I'll get it.

EMILY: And my PE kit.

MICHELLE: Aye, okay! Get out Emily.
                *(Michelle grabs Emily's bag as they both
                exit.)*

MICHELLE: *(Off-stage)*

                Right. Cheers Marie – see you later girls.

                (Michelle enters and sits on the couch.)

MICHELLE: For fucks – School run, done! Six hours of
                peace, thank fuck. That was Emily by the
                way – my youngest, and she's the worst of
                them both, a right wee cheeky shite. All
                they think I do is sit on this couch and
                vegetate. When in reality I'm actually
                slaving away in this House all day on my
                day off. With the amount of shite and
                rubbish that a pull out a they two fannies'
                bedrooms, now I use fannies as a term of
                endearment, but the amount of shite that
                that I pull out from their rooms is enough to
                fill every single bin on this estate – sixteen
                bags of crisps – that's what a pulled out
                from behind Emily's mattress, it's fuckin'
                rank. You wouldn't think that they both
                have bins in their rooms. No, it's too
                fuckin' easy to stuff all that rubbish down
                the side of their fuckin' mattresses. Fuckin'
                reprobates – again, a term of endearment. I
                still can't believe that I managed to birth

                             5

two manky kids. Well, I best get started on all this they've left me to clean up but I mean it's just the biggest thrill of my life and I just don't know where to start.

(Blackout)

(As the lights come up – Michelle is still sitting on the couch, yet the room is a lot tidier.)

MICHELLE: Six loads of washing, done. Dishes, done. Hooverin', done. Everything, done – and all done with what? Three minutes to spare until Thing One and Thing Two come home. Three minutes till they get home, and then a hour until the Ginger Prick comes to pick them up for the weekend. Pure fuckin' bliss.

EMILY: *(Off-stage)* Thanks Marie. See you next week.

(Farrah and Emily enter.)

FARRAH: God…

EMILY: She's so annoying.

MICHELLE: What?

FARRAH: Marie.

6

EMILY: So annoying.

MICHELLE: Shut it. Marie's lovely. Now don't touch anything – it took me all day to get this House in order.

            (Emily bursts a packet of crisps on the floor.)

            For fucks –

EMILY: Sorry…

MICHELLE: Hoover. Now.

EMILY: Aye. Okay.

            (Emily continues to eat the rest of the crisps in the bag.)

FARRAH: What are we getting to eat?

MICHELLE: Whatever your Dad gets you.

FARRAH: What?

MICHELLE: Get a packet of crisps like fuckin' Chucky from The Rugrats over there.

EMILY: Oi.

FARRAH: Jesus Christ.

MICHELLE: Phone your Dad and tell him to hurry up, I

	can't be dealing' with you two.
EMILY:	Sounds like you want rid of us.
MICHELLE:	Listen – I love you both more than anything on this entire planet but I think I love the peace and quiet a little bit more.
FARRAH:	Charming.
EMILY:	None taken.
MICHELLE:	Shut it Chucky.
EMILY:	I swear to God, you're getting' put in a shite care home.
MICHELLE:	Fucking try it.
FARRAH:	Mum, where did you put that drink?
MICHELLE:	In the fridge but listen, come here and sit down.
EMILY:	Can I go to the party?
MICHELLE & FARRAH:	No!

(Farrah sits down next to Michelle.)

| MICHELLE: | Listen, Farrah. This is your first party. |

8

FARRAH: Oh God.

MICHELLE: What?

FARRAH: Here we go, with 'The Talk'.

MICHELLE: Listen, you don't need to get totally wasted.
             You can enjoy the party just the same if
             you're sober as you would if you were
             drunk.

FARRAH: Okay.

MICHELLE: So, rule number one: be back at your Dad's
             by twelve. Number two: don't get too
             drunk. Number three: No drugs – I swear
             Farrah, I will kill you if you take anything.
             And lastly, phone me when you get back to
             your Dad's tonight. I'll be waiting.

FARRAH: Jesus Christ.

MICHELLE: Farrah, I'm serious. Phone me or I'll turn
             up on your Dad's doorstep.

FARRAH: I know, I know.

MICHELLE: Good.

FARRAH: Twelve though? Seriously?

MICHELLE: Do you want to go at all?

EMILY: Dad's here. He's early.

MICHELLE: It's not the first time that your Dad's been early Hun.

EMILY: Can a get a tenner?

MICHELLE: No. Now, come here.

              (Pulls Emily in for hug.)

              I love you.

EMILY: Love you too.

MICHELLE: Right. Beat it; phone me before you go to bed. Love you.

              (Emily exits.)

FARRAH: See you later, Mum.

MICHELLE: Wait there. Come here.

              (Michelle hugs Farrah.)

              Stay safe, enjoy yourself and remember to phone me.

FARRAH: I know, don't get too drunk, home by twelve, no drugs and phone you.

MICHELLE: Good girl. Remember, I love you.

FARRAH: Love you too.

              (Farrah exits.)

MICHELLE : Finally, peace and fucking quiet.

              (Michelle sits on the couch and pours a glass of wine.)

MICHELLE: Peace and fuckin' quiet.

              (Blackout)

              (As the lights come back up, Michelle is asleep on the couch. Her ringing phone wakes her up.)

              Hello?

              Peter?

              Hold up.

              What's the matter?

              (Panicking)

              Is she drunk? What do you mean her face is blue?

              The paramedics are on their way?

              Listen, you fuckin' stay with her. Send Emily to her room. Am on my way.

(Michelle exits.)

THREE
Michelle and Emily's House

(Michelle enters. Visibly distraught.)

MICHELLE: *(To the audience)* Hello.
Hello again. I really don't know how to say
this but someone should tell you all. My
baby, Farrah passed away this morning. I
didn't even want her to go to that stupid
party. Farrah really wanted to be a forensic
scientist and now, I'll never get to see my
baby girl go to University, I'll never see her
walk down the aisle, I'll never hold her
children in my arms. This feels like a
nightmare that I'm never going to wake up
from. We might never see Farrah again but
she will never be without us and we, we
will never be without her. Farrah brought so
much happiness to us all and now, her life
has been tragically cut short due to an
illness that we never even knew that she
suffered from – Long QT syndrome, an
irregular heartbeat. I will never understand
it and I don't think anyone will ever
understand it. I'm going to miss my baby so
much! Her heart simply stopped beating,
but now mine must beat for the both of us.

(Blackout.)

FOUR

(Tayla is reading a newspaper.)

(Throughout the scene Michelle and Emily don't acknowledge any of the other cast. Neither do Matt and Tayla but they both interact with each other.)

TAYLA: Here, Matt – listen to this. "A school has paid tribute to a teenage girl who died after possibly taking an "ecstasy-type drug" at a house party in South Lanarkshire. Farrah Mitchell, sixteen, fell ill and later died after attending the party in Rutherglen on Friday night. Her school, Eastbank Academy, in Shettleston, Glasgow, said Farrah was popular and her death was tragic news. Police said further tests were needed to determine if Farrah died as a result of taking drugs or from natural causes. It is understood that the results of a post-mortem examination have not been received yet. Members of Farrah's family are also said to believe that she may have died from a heart condition.

MATT: What? Let me see!

(Matt takes the newspaper from her.)

TAYLA: What the fuck?

MATT: An ecstasy-type drug?

14

TAYLA: Farrah never touched drugs in her entire
            life.

MATT: I know. Farrah didn't even drink.

TAYLA: What are we going to do?

            (Matt and Tayla exit.)

            (Michelle enters.)

MICHELLE: An ecstasy-type drug. I can't believe this.
            My baby hasn't even been gone a week and
            her name's already been dragged through
            every tabloid in Glasgow. The Evening
            Times, The Sun, and The Star – she was
            even on the front cover of the Daily Record.
            It's fucking horrible seeing my baby's
            pictures plastered over that shite quality
            paper with lies plastered next to her picture.
            Lies about my baby girl that everyone in the
            whole fuckin' country has seen. It's just not
            fair. Farrah was a model school student. She
            was polite, she was thoughtful and kind and
            now, now she's gone and all we have left to
            remember her is her memory. And now
            these articles with my baby's picture
            plastered all over them. Hours after her
            death, the police issued a false statement
            relating her death to drugs – this is wrong.
            My family have been subjected to vile
            Internet taunts mocking my daughter.
            Branding her a 'druggie' and a 'junkie'.

Police Scotland should have never said that before they were sure of the circumstances. I'm sure they thought, party. Sixteen years old. It's got to be drugs! But there was no evidence of that. There was no evidence for this. My daughter's name has been tarnished and there was no evidence. How can they have jumped to that conclusion so quickly? It's no fair on anyone, not me, not my family and not my daughter who isn't here to defend herself. I'm sure they will say it was their duty of care but they have run my daughter's name in the ground. A sorry from them will never be good enough. They cannot take this back – they have obliterated and destroyed everything Farrah was and is. Her death was NOT drug related.

(Lights go down on Michelle and come back up on Matt and Tayla.)

MATT: I can't believe it. Fifteen newspapers. All with Farrah in them. And all of them, lies. Here, listen to the Daily Mail: A teenage girl was last night feared to have become Scotland's youngest female victim of a killer ecstasy-style party drug. Farrah Mitchell, 16, is thought to have taken the drug at a house party in Rutherglen, Lanarkshire, on Friday night, attended by about 50 people. She was unwell when she returned home and died several hours later, prompting a police inquiry. Last night, a

senior officer warned of the dangers of the
drug, which is rapidly regaining popularity.

TAYLA: This is bullshit.

MATT: It goes on. "Farrah's death appears to be the
            latest in a series of drug-related fatalities in
            recent months, caused by ecstasy or so-
            called 'legal highs' that replicate the effects
            of drugs. Farrah is understood to have taken
            an ecstasy-type tablet at the party on Friday
            night. She returned home feeling unwell at
            around 5am and died several hours later."

TAYLA: Understood? It is not understood that Farrah
            took an E.

MATT: They're just lying at this point. None of it
            even mentions that she has,

            (Beat)

            Had a heart condition.

TAYLA: You just said…

MATT: I know, it just doesn't feel real.

TAYLA: I know, it's only been a day; it'll take some
            getting used to.

MATT: I don't want it to be real.

TAYLA: It seems like just yesterday she was…

MATT: It was.

             (Emily enters.)

EMILY: Life just has to be so cruel sometimes. My
             sister has been ripped away and I just don't
             understand. When her heart stopped
             beating, mine was ripped in two. I miss you
             Farrah. I miss you with all of my heart.
             Nothing seems to be right, nothing is
             though – you're not here. Nothing will ever
             be right again. I'd give anything for one
             more argument. I'd give anything for just
             one second longer with you. Nothing in this
             world could ever replace what we've all
             lost. I miss you shouting at me for drinking
             the last bottle of Lucozade. It's weird just
             being able to go in the bathroom without
             you hogging it; it's weird having enough
             hot water in the boiler to actually get a
             decent amount of time in the bathroom.
             Life's just weird right now Farrah, and I
             know that you would be the only person
             that would have the answers to all of the
             questions swimming around inside of my
             head right now. And that's the worst part of
             it. That I can't go to anyone right now. I
             don't understand why you had to go Farrah.
             We all needed you here. You were the rock
             of the family, everyone thought that we
             looked after you but in fact, it was you that

looked after us. There are no longer cracks in our family, it's just shattered. And I don't think anything will ever be able to fix it Farrah. Nothing.

(Michelle enters.)

MICHELLE: I mean, I would be able to understand it if it wasn't my daughter. I'd be heartbroken but I might have been able to understand. I'd have understood if it were me that had died. No parent should ever have to bury their daughter. Everything is just empty. Empty except for Emily. I don't think I'd have survived this if it weren't for her. She's the only light left in this world now. Well, the only light left in my world.

MATT: This can't be legal.

TAYLA: What?

MATT: I swear. This cannot be legal. The way they're just lying about Farrah. Surely it's not allowed.

TAYLA: I mean, surely it has to be legal or they wouldn't be able to print it.

(Beat)

I don't know. It's just wrong.

EMILY: I just don't know why anyone would think that this is fair. To pull someone so young away from their life. From their family – from the rest of their life. I just don't think I'll ever be able to understand why this happened. I love my sister. I loved my sister.

MICHELLE: I don't think anything can ever repair what's happened to my family, it's been ripped apart. One half in this world, the other in the next. I appreciate everyone who's spreading messages of love for Farrah and people keep saying doesn't that make you feel better? And the answer is…

EMILY: No, it doesn't make me feel better.

MICHELLE: It feels good.

EMILY: But nothing could make me feel better right now.

MICHELLE: Because I know they're just trying to make me feel better but all they are doing is listing off things about my daughter that everyone already knew.

EMILY: It's only comforting to know that Farrah was loved by so many people.

(All characters begin reading posts about Farrah from their phones.)

MATT: Farrah was the kindest person, I'd ever met.

MICHELLE: You'll be missed dearly.

TAYLA: Gone but never forgotten.

MATT: I'll miss you so much.

MICHELLE: I'll miss your laugh.

EMILY: I love you.

TAYLA: How has this happened?

MICHELLE: Spread your wings and fly high.

MATT: My thoughts are with Michelle and Emily.

EMILY: This is the stuff of fantasy books, my heart is broken.

TAYLA: I'll miss your smile.

EMILY: Rest in peace, princess.

MATT: RIP.

MICHELLE: I can't believe this is happening.

TAYLA:	Love you endlessly and miss you always.
EMILY:	Sleep tight my girl.
MICHELLE:	I can't imagine what her family are going through.
EMILY:	This is the hardest thing that I've ever had to write.
TAYLA:	I can't believe I have to write this.
MICHELLE:	I never thought Farrah would be gone so soon.
EMILY:	She was still a baby.
MICHELLE:	Such an amazing girl with her whole life ahead of her.
MATT:	The world is missing an amazing young woman.
EMILY:	A model pupil, a role model.
MATT:	Farrah wouldn't touch drugs.
TAYLA:	She didn't even like to drink.
EMILY:	So tragic.

MATT: I can't believe this has happened.

MICHELLE: A credit to her family.

TAYLA: Michelle, we all know the papers are lying.

EMILY: We all know that journalists have a
               tendency to lie.

MICHELLE: Michelle, don't take any notice.

MATT: We know that it's not true.

ALL: We know that it's not true

TAYLA: As Farrah would say.

EMILY: No point in crying.

MICHELLE: So may as well smile.

MATT: No point in crying, so may as well smile.

TAYLA: No point in crying, so may as well smile.

EMILY: No point in crying, so may as well smile.

MICHELLE: No point in crying, so may as well smile.

EMILY: No point in crying.

ALL: So may as well smile.

TAYLA: Farrah was a junkie.

ALL: LIES.

MATT: Farrah isn't really dead.

ALL: LIES.

TAYLA: Farrah is just hiding somewhere, too
            embarrassed cause she was popping pills.

ALL: LIES.

EMILY: LIES ABOUT MY SISTER.

TAYLA: LIES ABOUT MY FRIEND.

MICHELLE: LIES ABOUT MY DAUGHTER.

MATT: LIES ABOUT MY FRIEND.

ALL: LIES PRINTED IN NATIONAL
            NEWSPAPERS.

MICHELLE: Do you ever get to that point where you just
            want to smash everything up? I'm sick of it
            all, I don't want to be in a world without my
            daughter. I don't want to be in a world
            where I'm waiting on the post mortem to
            come back so I can prove that my daughter
            didn't take drugs. I don't want to be in a

world that's suddenly so dark without her in it.

EMILY: I want my sister back.

TAYLA &
MATT: We want our friend back.

MICHELLE: I want the newspapers to stop printing lies about my daughter.

FIVE
Michelle and Emily's House

NEWS REPORTER: *(Voice over.)*	Hello. And welcome to the STV news at six. It is currently reported that a teenage girl from the East End of Glasgow has died due to taking a supposed ecstasy-type drug. The mother of the daughter has denied these claims stating, 'my daughter has never touched drugs'. More on this story later in the show.
EMILY:	STV news. That's a national news station and now they're liars too.
MICHELLE:	Turn that off.
EMILY:	Mum.
MICHELLE:	Emily I will not ask you again. Turn it off.
EMILY:	I just wanted to see her again.
MICHELLE:	I know.
EMILY:	I miss her Mum.
MICHELLE:	I know you do.
EMILY:	Why?
MICHELLE:	Why, what?

EMILY: Why did this happen to us? To her?

MICHELLE: I don't know baby.

EMILY: It's not fair Mum.

               (There is a knock at the door.)

MICHELLE: Go and see who that is.

               (Emily goes to the door.)

NEWS
REPORTER: Hi. Hello. Is there a Miss Miller here? I'm
(Off-stage)   Joanne. I'm a reporter from the Daily Mail.

EMILY: Erm. Mum.
(Off-stage)

MICHELLE: What?

EMILY: It's a reporter.
(Off-stage)
MICHELLE: WHAT?

               (Emily and the News Reporter enter.)

               NEWS REPORTER: Hi, my name is
               Joanne Carter. I'm a senior journalist at the
               Daily Mail.

MICHELLE: You've got some nerve coming here after

what you've done to my family.

NEWS
REPORTER: Miss Miller.

MICHELLE: Michelle.

NEW
REPORTER: Michelle. We have received notification
            from Police Scotland that our reports were
            incorrect, well slightly.

EMILY: SLIGHTLY?

NEWS
REPORTER: We only reported that it was suspected.

MICHELLE: You should have never have even put my
            daughter's name in the same sentence as
            that word.

NEWS
REPORTER: Miss Miller. We have been told that there
            has now been a conclusive report that your
            daughter did not have drugs in her system
            at the time of her death.

EMILY: At the time of ever. My sister didn't take
            drugs. Ever.

NEWS

REPORTER: I am here to offer our most sincere apologies. I understand that this must have been a traumatic experience for your family.

MICHELLE: No shit.

NEWS
REPORTER: We are sorry.

MICHELLE: Sorry will never be good enough. Wait, you said there is conclusive evidence?

NEWS
REPORTER: A report.

MICHELLE: Are you telling me that my Daughter's post mortem has come back and no one has told me?

NEWS
REPORTER: Erm.

MICHELLE: Tell me! This is my daughter you're talking about!

NEWS
REPORTER: You really must speak to the police Miss Miller.

MICHELLE: Get out.

NEWS

REPORTER: Sorry?

MICHELLE: GET OUT OF MY HOUSE. YOUR SHIT
NEWSPAPER PRINTED LIES ABOUT
MY BABY AND NOW YOU'RE
STANDING HERE TELLING ME
YOU'RE SORRY CAUSE YOU WERE
WRONG AND THAT YOU HAVE SEEN
MY DAUGHTER'S POST MORTEM
REPORT BEFORE I HAVE. GET OUT
OF MY HOUSE. I NEVER WANT TO
SEE YOU AGAIN.

NEWS
REPORTER: We really are sorry.

MICHELLE: GET OUT OF MY HOUSE.

NEWS
REPORTER: Thank you for your time – I'm sorry for
your loss.

(The News Reporter exits.)

MICHELLE: Emily go to your room.

EMILY: But…

MICHELLE: Emily I said go to your room, now.

(Emily exits.)

(Michelle picks up her phone and dials a

30

number.)

Hello. Is this Shettleston Police Station?

(Beat)

Yes. I would like to talk to PC Elliott regarding the Farrah Mitchell case.

(Beat)

Yes. I'll hold.

(Beat)

Of course PC Elliott isn't available to talk on the phone at the moment. You tell him that Michelle Miller is on her way to the Station and tell him I won't be leaving until I speak to him.

(Michelle hangs up the phone.)

Emily!

(Emily enters.)

EMILY: What did they say?

MICHELLE: Put your shoes on.

EMILY: What did they say?

MICHELLE: Will you just do as I tell you. For once,

31

please.

(Beat)

MICHELLE: Come on. Let's go. Get in the car.

(They both exit.)

SIX
The Police Station

(Michelle and Emily enter the police station. The desk is unmanned.)

MICHELLE: Go sit down, Emily.

(Emily sits on the seats by the desk.)

Hello is anyone there?

(PC Henderson enters.)

PC
HENDERSON: Hello. How can I help you?

MICHELLE: Hi, it's Michelle Miller, I need to speak with PC Elliott as a matter of urgency.

PC
HENDERSON: Can I ask what it's regarding?

MICHELLE: Farrah Mitchell.

PC
HENDERSON: Okie dokie. Just let me go and see if he is available.

MICHELLE: I'm not leaving until I speak with him.

PC
HENDERSON: I'll let him know. Please take a seat.

(Looks to Emily)

Can I help you?

MICHELLE: She's with me.

(Michelle sits down.)

(PC Henderson exits.)

SEVEN

MATT: Hey.

TAYLA: Did you hear?

MATT: About the funeral?

TAYLA: I can't believe it's gonna be another two days before they release her body. I don't like the idea of her sitting in some cold morgue.

MATT: It's really starting to sink in now.

TAYLA: I know.

MATT: Today was the worst. I walked into Science and someone had put a textbook on her desk. I think that's when it hit me.

TAYLA: It hit me when I found this.

                     (Tayla shows Matt a birthday card.)

MATT: What is it?

TAYLA: The last birthday card she bought me. I don't know why I kept it.

MATT: She'd be glad you did.

TAYLA: Fuck me, I miss her so much.

MATT: It's been three days yet it feels like a lifetime.

TAYLA: This time last week she was still here. We were planning what we were gonna do over the summer, and now...

MATT: We could do all those things.

TAYLA: What?

MATT: I mean we could do everything you two planned, you know like one last goodbye. It'd be nice to do something nice in her memory.

TAYLA: I guess so.

MATT: I mean if you don't think it's a good idea.

TAYLA: No, I do.

MATT: What's the first thing on the list?

TAYLA: The Time Capsule.

MATT: Really?

TAYLA: We haven't been for ages we were just gonna go.

MATT: Fine. Next Saturday – we're going to the Time Capsule. Bring your swimming goggles.

TAYLA: She'd have loved doing all of these
            things.

MATT: Well, maybe every time we do something
            we should take some of her with us.

TAYLA: What do you mean?

MATT: We could like a picture of her. You know
            so she's doing them all with us.

TAYLA: How're you coping?

MATT: I don't know. Honestly, I don't know.

TAYLA: You know, she always thought you were
            cute.

MATT: What?

TAYLA: She thought you were cute.

MATT: Fuck me; she was funny when she
            wanted to be.

TAYLA: What?

MATT: She was like my sister.

TAYLA: True. I wonder what she'd make of all
            this. The newspapers.

MATT: She'll be laughing up there. Still causing trouble after she's gone.

TAYLA: Do you remember in primary school, at Castle Toward when she fell over during the mud run?

MATT: Do I remember? I don't think she managed to get the mud out of her hair for the whole week.

TAYLA: And when she managed to fill four sick bags on the bus home.

MATT: I don't think Miss Hay was impressed.

TAYLA: Miss Hay? I don't think anyone was impressed! It was a hot summers day and she made the whole bus stink!

MATT: God. It's mental.

TAYLA: What?

MATT: That we'll never have any more memories like that with her. It's not fair.

TAYLA: I know.

(Blackout)

EIGHT
The Police Station

(PC Elliott enters.)

PC ELLIOTT: Hello. Mrs Miller?

MICHELLE: Miss.

PC ELLIOTT: What can I assist you with today?

MICHELLE: I'd like to know why you thought that it would be more appropriate to give the press the results of my daughter's post mortem before you gave them to me?

PC ELLIOTT: Ah. If you'd like to follow me into one of the interview rooms?

MICHELLE: Why?

PC ELLIOTT: Michelle…

MICHELLE: Why? So that people don't know how much a fuck up this whole Police force has been?

PC ELLIOTT: Please.

MICHELLE: Please what? Please be quiet? Please don't make a scene? I'm sorry my daughter is dead. I will make a scene if I like!

39

(Blackout)

NINE

NEWS
REPORTER: Hello, and welcome back to Live at Five
(Voice over)   on STV. The case of Farrah Mitchell has
now escalated as the teenage girl's post
mortem results have been disclosed to the
press. It was thought that the teenager
had died after taking an ecstasy-type drug
however the post mortem results
conclude that the teenager died after
suffering from an undisclosed and
previously unnoticed heart problem
known as Long QT.

TEN
The Police Station Interview Room

PC ELLIOTT: I really hope what we have discussed with you today has really helped you Miss Miller.

MICHELLE: Helped? Are you being serious? You gave the press the results of my daughter's post mortem before I had them. Nothing could help this.

PC ELLIOTT: Again, all I can do is apologise.

MICHELLE: Too little, too late.

(Beat)

Thank you for your time Officer. Come on Emily, let's go.

PC ELLIOTT: Have a good day.

(Michelle and Emily exit.)

ELEVEN

MATT: Are you going tomorrow?

TAYLA: To see her?

MATT: Yeah.

TAYLA: I don't know.

MATT: I don't know if I can.

TAYLA: I don't know if that's how I want to remember her. You know, like the last time that we ever see her.

MATT: I've never seen anyone like…

TAYLA: Dead?

MATT: No.

TAYLA: Me neither.

MATT: I wanted to see my Grandma, but my Mum thought I was too young.

TAYLA: That's what happened when my Aunty died.

MATT: I dunno. I just feel like the last time we saw her she was just so full of life and…

TAYLA: I know.

MATT: Thank you.

TAYLA: What?

MATT: I don't know what I'd have done without
             you, you know.

TAYLA: I mean I know it still doesn't feel right
             just the two of us, I mean we're so used
             to it being the three of us but I feel like
             this is the closest to any amount of
             normality that we will be able to come to
             in all of this.

MATT: It feels right, if that makes sense. I don't
             want to be with anyone else at the
             moment. I just don't want to answer
             anyone else's questions.

TAYLA: No one else gets it.

MATT: Well, to be honest – I don't even think
             that we get it.

TAYLA: I don't think we ever will.

MATT: You know, I think we should go
             tomorrow. She was our best friend and I
             just don't want to regret not going to see
             her.

             (Beat)

	I mean, other than the funeral, this is the last time that we can really say goodbye.
TAYLA:	I don't know.
MATT:	I won't go if you don't want to.
TAYLA:	Don't let me stop you.
MATT:	No, I'm not going without you. It wouldn't really feel right.
TAYLA:	Let's go.
MATT:	Are you sure?
TAYLA:	No.
MATT:	You don't need to. I mean, if you don't want to.
TAYLA:	I don't know.
MATT:	We can just go at your own pace.
TAYLA:	Thank you.
MATT:	I love you, you know that? You've really saved me these past few days.
TAYLA:	It's crazy. Sitting under the stars like this. She'd have loved it.

44

MATT: She is one of the stars now.

TAYLA: You think?

MATT: The brightest one.

               (Tayla kisses Matt.)

TWELVE
A Chapel of Rest

               *(There is a coffin in the middle of the
               stage on trestles.)*

MICHELLE: I can't believe we're laying you to rest
               tomorrow. It's all starting to feel real
               now baby. I miss you, but – you know
               that, don't you? We all know that you're
               up there watching over us all. The house
               has been so quiet. We just want all of this
               to be a crazy nightmare Farrah. I want to
               read you something – I want to read you
               what I'm going to say tomorrow at the
               Church, I want your seal of approval.
               (Exhales and pulls out a piece of paper.)
               Here go's nothing. I want to thank
               everyone for coming. Farrah would have
               loved this! All of this love and these
               people gathered here to say goodbye to
               her. Farrah loved you all, and she
               would've loved being the centre of
               attention right now. I wish it wasn't
               happening though. I know she'll be
               looking down on us and saying. " Oh no,
               Mum. Sit down – you're embarrassing

                          45

me. You're using that awful posh phone voice and your bound to cry and say something totally stupid about me. Someone stop her!" You know, she once said to me after she got into trouble in Primary School, "Mum, I've caused you so much trouble, I bet you wish I'd never been born." She couldn't have been further from the truth. Goodbye, my precious girl – I know you're up there now, waving down to us, your smile beaming the brightest of us all. I love you my baby girl. Sleep tight. I'll see you tomorrow baby girl, I love you.

(Michelle exits.)

THIRTEEN
Farrah's Funeral

> *(There is a coffin in the middle of the stage on trestles with a picture of Farrah on top of it.)*

MATT: It can never be fair.

TAYLA: To rip someone so young away from their life.

MATT: From what they had ahead of them.

TAYLA: From the memories they could've made.

MATT: From the memories that we could have made.

TAYLA: It's unfair that someone so young will never grow old.

MATT: It's unfair that someone so young will never see her eighteenth birthday.

TAYLA: I miss her smile.

MATT: I miss the smell of her perfume.

TAYLA: Angel. Thierry Mugler.

MATT: I miss her laugh.

MATT & TAYLA:	I miss her.
TAYLA:	She was always there when I needed her.
MATT:	When we needed her.
TAYLA:	When I needed a shoulder to lean on.
MATT:	When I was feeling down.
TAYLA:	She was there.
MATT:	And now.
TAYLA:	Now.
MATT:	She's gone.
TAYLA:	Farrah was our best friend.
MATT:	We were inseparable.
TAYLA:	Our Drama Teacher called us 'The Supremes.'
MATT:	I love writing.
TAYLA:	And I love singing.
MATT:	But Farrah loved reading, and poetry.
TAYLA:	And today, we want to read you a poem

in memory of her.

MATT: The depths of infinity by Shilow.

TAYLA: The depths of infinity.

MATT: Of ancient wisdom.

TAYLA: And comic mystery.

MATT: Coursing through our veins.

TAYLA: While the centres of atoms explode.

MATT: In and out of time.

TAYLA: Where are we when we fall between breaths.

MATT: When we slip through the cracks.

TAYLA: Of space time.

MATT: Like oozing molasses.

TAYLA: Slowly dripping.

MATT: Never stopping, the yearning of our hearts.

TAYLA: That will never give up.

MATT: We are always held up.

TAYLA:	By those dramatic atoms.
MATT:	Diving deep through intelligence.
TAYLA:	That rotates stars.
MATT:	And beats our hearts.
TAYLA:	To pop back in time.
MATT:	Back into our dimension.
TAYLA:	As a new dimension.
MATT:	Of who we are.
TAYLA:	Our best friend was simply that.
MATT:	A best friend.
TAYLA:	When you needed a pick me up…
MATT:	She was there to make you fly.
TAYLA:	She wasn't a user.
MATT:	Or an abuser. Like the newspapers have made out.
TAYLA:	Farrah was kind, compassionate and caring. And never deserved for this to happen.
MATT:	We will fight for her, because she can't.

We won't give up until her face is on the front of every newspaper with an apology attached.

TAYLA: Because she was ours to remember and not their story to share.

MATT: Farrah. We miss you.

TAYLA: Always and forever.

(Blackout)

(The funeral has ended. Matt and Tayla are standing by Farrah's coffin. Michelle enters.)

MICHELLE: That was beautiful.

TAYLA: Thank you.
MICHELLE: What you did today, for Farrah – I'll never be able to repay.

MATT: We don't need repaid.

TAYLA: We did it for her.

MATT: And what we said, about fighting for her – we meant it. We won't stop until the whole world knows how she went.

TAYLA: How's Emily?

MICHELLE: Holding up, I mean, it's been a rough day for us all. You two should go home, you done our girl proud today.

MATT: Erm, Michelle. We kinda wanted to run something by you.

TAYLA: Matt?

MICHELLE: Yes, buddy?

MATT: We didn't want to say anything cause it's been a rough week. But Tayla and I, we've connected more than we ever have and well –

(Matt takes Tayla's hand.)

MICHELLE: You're together.

TAYLA: This is why I didn't want to tell you –

MICHELLE: Thank fuck for that…

TAYLA: What?

MICHELLE: I was starting to think he was gay. I'm not gonna lie to you.

(They all laugh.)

MICHELLE: Listen, this world is a hard and cruel place. And you have to find happiness wherever you can. I'm happy for you both.

MATT: Really?

MICHELLE: Yes, really! I love you both so very much
            – you've helped get me Daughter's name
            back, you deserve to be happy. Now
            come on, I'll drop you both off.

            (They all exit.)

FOURTEEN

MICHELLE: *(To the Audience)* Hello, today it finally happened something I've been waiting two years for. It's been two years since my daughter died. Two years since my baby's picture was flashed all over the news – 'Scotland's youngest ecstasy death'. Police Scotland fucked up, and finally they admitted it. Do you know how good that feels? To finally have everyone know the truth. I've waited for what seems like a lifetime for this to happen. Two years later and Farrah's still causing a stir. It finally feels good, you know – I kind of feel like I'm at peace, not totally cause you know, nothing will ever bring Farrah back but something just feels like I can finally properly mourn my daughter. Whereas last time I was more focused on maintaining that my daughter wasn't a drug user. I had to be strong for Emily, I still do but I feel like now I'm allowed to cry, I feel like I am allowed to grieve my daughter. It's still so crazy, I still hear her, and sometimes, I see her in my dreams. Everything goes back to normal; I mean, we're all arguing over the amount of hot water in the boiler, I miss it. Happy 19th Birthday Farrah baby, I love you.

(Emily enters.)

54

EMILY: Mum, are you okay?

MICHELLE: I'm fine.

EMILY: It's today isn't it?

MICHELLE: What?

EMILY: Her birthday.

            (Michelle nods her head.)

EMILY: Why are you sad?

MICHELLE: I miss her.

EMILY: So do I.

MICHELLE: I know, baby – I know.

EMILY: Sometimes it feels like everyone has forgotten her, you know?

MICHELLE: I know.

EMILY: Like everyone has just moved on with their lives and left her in the past.

            (Beat)

            I don't want my sister to be left in the past. She's been gone for two years, Mum. Two years. Seven hundred and thirty days. When you say it like that it feels like no time at all yet the atoms in the entire world have changed. Nothing is the same, everything has changed since she took her last breath, it's almost like everything is moving too fast. Life is going too fast, I want it slow down. I don't want my sister's memory to be lost. I just don't want it to happen, I don't, I don't, I don't.

MICHELLE: Sometimes that's what happens though baby, I miss her too. More than anyone could ever imagine.

EMILY: I can imagine.

MICHELLE: I know.

EMILY: Something is missing. It was like time should have stopped and we should have waited until things seemed right again but it kept going; it should have stood still. The world should have stopped spinning on it's axis.

MICHELLE: I know, baby.

EMILY: I'm tired of it. I'm tired of people seeing me in the corridors of school. Simply smiling at me because my sister died. The day she died I wasn't Emily. I was Farrah's sister, or the girl whose sister died. People literally tiptoe around me because they think that they're going to upset me. I just sometimes think I'm something that people are too scared to break, when in reality, I'm fine. I'm cool. Yes, I miss my sister. Yes, it breaks my heart that I'll never get to see her again but I am just a normal human being and yes, I have feelings and yes, sometimes some things upset me. Walking past Farrah's locker every day in school – that chokes me up, knowing that my sister kept her stuff in there. But people being too scared to upset me that upsets me too. I just want to be a normal human being. I don't want to be known as just 'Farrah's Sister', I mean I'll always be Farrah's sister but I am me too, I don't want to be, I never wanted to be 'that girl whose sister died'. I want to go back to being Emily. I want to go back to the time where me and my sister would fight over who had the hairbrush last, that's what breaks my heart knowing that people who don't even deserve to be happy still have their whole family to love and cherish them yet ours has been ripped apart. I don't want to be here anymore

MICHELLE: What do you mean?

EMILY: Sometimes the world just doesn't seem worth it anymore. You know.

MICHELLE: EMILY! Don't ever say that again.

EMILY: Sometimes it just feels like the world is fighting against me – not running with me.

MICHELLE: Emily, no one is fighting against you.

EMILY: Sometimes it feels like it.

                (Beat)

                Sometimes it feels like there is no one in my corner.

MICHELLE: Hey! I will always be in your corner.

EMILY: I love you, Mum.

MICHELLE: I love you too. Always and forever, until the end of time.

EMILY: I'm glad you're still here.

MICHELLE: What?

EMILY: I'm glad you're still here. I'd miss you a lot.

MICHELLE: I'm not going anywhere. But you are.

EMILY: What?

MICHELLE: Straight to bed, that's where you're
               going. You have school in the morning.

EMILY: Do I have to?

MICHELLE: Yes. Now go. Bed.

               (Emily exits.)

(To the
audience):   Did you just hear that? My baby thinks
               the world is against her. I've been so
               busy trying to get Farrah's name out of
               the papers that I've completely neglected
               Emily; I've just always expected her to
               be fine. She's just a little girl; she's had
               to deal with a lot more than anyone else
               her age and, to be honest – I don't know
               how she's dealt with it all. I don't know
               if she's just put on a brave face so that I
               would worry or if she really is just a
               strong cookie. Who am I kidding, she
               isn't a strong cookie, and she thinks that
               world is fighting against her.

FIFTEEN

NEWS
REPORTER:
(Voice-over.)

Hello, and welcome to the STV News at Six, it has just been reported that a teenage girl has passed away just two years after her older sister passed away. Emily Mitchell, a student who was preparing for her upcoming examinations passed away, the cause of death has been identified as Long QT syndrome, a condition that affects the repolarisation of the heart after a heartbeat – the same syndrome that killed her older sister, Farrah Mitchell two years ago. A source close to the family said, 'Emily's heart simply stopped beating, we know that she will be in Heaven now, reunited with her older sister. Like Farrah, Emily had her whole life ahead of her and tragedy has struck his family twice now.' Here at STV, we would like to express our thoughts of sympathy to the family

SIXTEEN

TAYLA: Stop all of the clocks, cut off the telephone. Prevent the dog from barking with a juicy bone. Silence the pianos and with muffled drum. Bring out the coffin and let the mourners come.

MATT: Let aeroplanes circle overhead. Scribbling on the sky, the message – she is dead. Put crepe bows around the public doves. Let the traffic policemen wear black cotton gloves.

MICHELLE: She was my North, my South, my East and West. My working week, and Sunday rest. Our noon, our midnight. Our talk, our song. I thought that friendship would last forever. I was wrong.

ALL: The stars are not wanted now; put out everyone. Pack up the moon and dismantle the sun. Pour away the ocean and sweep away the woods; For nothing now can ever come to any good.

TAYLA: W.H Auden.

(End of play.)

Printed in Great Britain
by Amazon